HORRiD
HENRY'S
NiTS

Francesca Simon is an American who lives
in London with her English husband and
her son. She grew up in California, was
educated at Yale and Oxford Universities,
and was a freelance journalist, writing theatre
and restaurant reviews for some years. She
is now a very successful writer of children's
books, ranging from picture books to young
fiction.

Also by Francesca Simon

HORRID HENRY'S NITS

Francesca Simon

Illustrated by Tony Ross

Orion
Children's Books

For my dear friend
Dearbhla Molloy

ORION CHILDREN'S BOOKS

First published in Great Britain in 1997 by Orion Children's Books
This edition published in 2016 by Hodder and Stoughton

7

A CIP catalogue record for this book
is available from the British Library.

ISBN 978 1 4072 3047 4

Printed and bound in Great Britain
by Clays Ltd, St Ives plc

The paper and board used in this book are
made from wood from responsible sources.

MIX
Paper from
responsible sources
FSC® C104740

Orion Children's Books
An imprint of
Hachette Children's Group
Part of Hodder and Stoughton
Carmelite House
50 Victoria Embankment
London EC4Y 0DZ

An Hachette UK Company
www.hachette.co.uk

www.hachettechildrens.co.uk

CONTENTS

1

HORRID HENRY'S NITS

Scratch. Scratch. Scratch.

Dad scratched his head.

"Stop scratching, please," said Mum. "We're eating dinner."

Mum scratched her head.

"Stop scratching, please," said Dad. "We're eating dinner."

Henry scratched his head.

"Stop scratching, Henry!" said Mum and Dad.

"Uh-oh," said Mum. She put down her fork and frowned at Henry.

"Henry, do you have nits *again*?"

"Of course not," said Henry.

"Come over to the sink, Henry," said Mum.

"Why?" said Henry.

"I need to check your head."

Henry dragged his feet over to her as slowly as possible. It's not fair, he thought. It wasn't his fault nits loved him. Henry's head was a gathering place for nits far and wide. They probably held nit parties there and foreign nits visited him on their holidays.

Mum dragged the nit comb across Henry's head. She made a face and groaned.

"You're crawling with nits, Henry," said Mum.

"Ooh, let's see," said Henry. He always liked counting how many nits he had.

"One, two, three . . . forty-five, forty-six, forty-seven . . ." he counted, dropping them on to a paper towel.

"It's not polite to count nits," said his younger brother, Perfect Peter, wiping his mouth with his spotless napkin, "is it, Mum?"

"It certainly isn't," said Mum.

Dad dragged the nit comb across his head and made a face.

"Ughh," said Dad.

Mum dragged the comb through

her hair.

"Bleeeech," said Mum.

Mum combed Perfect Peter's hair. Then she did it again. And again. And again.

"No nits, Peter," said Mum, smiling. "As usual. Well done, darling."

Perfect Peter smiled modestly.

"It's because I wash and comb my hair every night," said Peter.

Henry scowled. True, his hair was filthy, but then . . .

"Nits love clean hair," said Henry.

"No they don't," said Peter. "*I've* never ever had nits."

We'll see about that, thought Henry. When no one was looking he picked a few nits off the paper towel. Then he wandered over to Peter and casually fingered a lock of his hair.

LEAP!

Scratch. Scratch.

"Mum!" squealed Peter. "Henry's pulling my hair!"

"Stop it, Henry," said Dad.

"I wasn't pulling his hair," said Henry indignantly. "I just wanted to see how clean it was. And it *is* so lovely and clean," added Henry sweetly. "I wish my hair was as clean as Peter's."

Peter beamed. It wasn't often that Henry said anything nice to him.

"Right," said Mum grimly, "everyone upstairs. It's shampoo time."

"NO!" shrieked Horrid Henry. "NO SHAMPOO!"

He hated the stinky smelly horrible shampoo much more than he hated having nits. Only today his teacher,

Miss Battle-Axe, had sent home a nit letter.

BEWARE!
NITS NITS NITS NITS
Nits have been seen
in school
GET RID OF THEM!
Wash your hair with
Supersonic NIT-
Blasting Shampoo
PLEASE —
OR ELSE.

Naturally, Henry had crumpled up the letter and thrown it away. He was never ever going to have pongy nit shampoo on his head again. What rotten luck Mum had spotted him scratching.

"It's the only way to get rid of nits," said Dad.

"But it never works!" screamed Henry. And he ran for the door.

Mum and Dad grabbed him. Then they dragged him kicking and screaming to the bathroom.

"Nits are living creatures," howled Henry. "Why kill them?"

"Because . . ." said Mum.

"Because . . . because . . . they're blood-sucking nits," said Dad.

Blood-sucking. Henry had never thought of that. In the split second that he stood still to consider this interesting information, Mum emptied the bottle of supersonic nit-blasting shampoo over his hair.

"NO!" screamed Henry. Frantically he shook his head. There was shampoo on the door. There was shampoo on the floor. There was shampoo all over Mum and Dad. The only place there was no shampoo was on Henry's head.

"Henry! Stop being horrid!" yelled Dad, wiping shampoo off his shirt.

"What a big fuss over nothing," said Peter.

Henry lunged at him. Mum seized Henry by the collar and held him back.

"Now Peter," said Mum. "That wasn't a kind thing to say to Henry, was it? Not everyone is as brave as you."

"You're right, Mum," said Perfect Peter. "I was being rude and thoughtless. It won't happen again. I'm so sorry, Henry."

Mum smiled at him. "That was a perfect apology, Peter. As for you, Henry . . ." she sighed. "We'll get more shampoo tomorrow."

Phew, thought Henry, giving his head an extra good scratch. Safe for one more day.

The next morning at school a group of parents burst into the classroom, waving the nit letter and shouting.

"My Margaret doesn't have nits!" shrieked Moody Margaret's mother.

"She never has and she never will. How dare you send home such a letter!"

"My Josh doesn't have nits," shouted his mother. "The idea!"

"My Toby doesn't have nits!" shouted his father. "Some nasty child in this class isn't bug-busting!"

Miss Battle-Axe squared her shoulders.

"Rest assured that the culprit will be found," she said. "I have declared war on nits."

Scratch. Scratch. Scratch.

Miss Battle-Axe spun round. Her beady eyes swivelled over the class.

"Who's scratching?" she demanded.

Silence.

Henry bent over his worksheet and tried to look studious.

"Henry is," said Moody Margaret.

"Liar!" shouted Horrid Henry. "It was William!"

Weepy William burst into tears.

"No it wasn't," he sobbed.

Miss Battle-Axe glared at the class.

"I'm going to find out once and for all who's got nits," she growled.

"I don't!" shouted Moody Margaret.

"I don't!" shouted Rude Ralph.

"I don't!" shouted Horrid Henry.

"Silence!" ordered Miss Battle-Axe. "Nora, the nit nurse, is coming this morning. Who's got nits? Who's not bug-busting? We'll all find out soon."

Uh-oh, thought Henry. Now I'm sunk. There was no escaping Nitty Nora Bug Explorer and her ferocious combs. Everyone would know *he* had the nits. Rude Ralph would never

stop teasing him. He'd be shampooed
every night. Mum and Dad would
find out about all the nit letters he'd
thrown away . . .

He could of course get a tummy
ache double quick and be sent home.
But Nitty Nora had a horrible way of
remembering whose head she hadn't
checked and then combing it in front
of the whole class.

He could run screaming out of the
door saying he'd caught mad cow
disease. But somehow he didn't think
Miss Battle-Axe would believe him.

There was no way out. This time
he was well and truly stuck.

Unless . . .

Suddenly Henry had a wonderful,
spectacular idea. It was so wicked,
and so horrible, that even Horrid
Henry hesitated. But only for a

moment. Desperate times call for desperate measures.

Henry leaned over Clever Clare and brushed his head lightly against hers.

LEAP!

Scratch. Scratch.

"Get away from me, Henry," hissed Clare.

"I was just admiring your lovely picture," said Henry.

He got up to sharpen his pencil. On his way to the sharpener he brushed against Greedy Graham.

LEAP!

Scratch. Scratch.

On his way back from the sharpener Henry stumbled and fell against Anxious Andrew.

LEAP!

Scratch. Scratch.

"Ow!" yelped Andrew.

"Sorry, Andrew," said Henry. "What big clumsy feet I have. Whoops!" he added, tripping over the carpet and banging heads with Weepy William.

LEAP!

Scratch. Scratch.

"Waaaaaaaaa!" wailed William.

"Sit down at once, Henry," said Miss Battle-Axe. "William! Stop scratching. Bert! How do you spell cat?"

"I dunno," said Beefy Bert.

Horrid Henry leaned across the table and put his head close to Bert's.

"C-A-T," he whispered helpfully.

LEAP!

Scratch. Scratch.

Then Horrid Henry raised his hand.

"Yes?" said Miss Battle-Axe.

"I don't understand these

instructions," said Henry sweetly. "Could you help me, please?"

Miss Battle-Axe frowned. She liked to keep as far away from Henry as possible. Reluctantly she came closer and bent over his work. Henry leaned his head near hers.

LEAP!

Scratch. Scratch.

There was a pounding at the door. Then Nitty Nora marched into the classroom, bristling with combs and other instruments of torture.

"Line up, everyone," said Miss Battle-Axe, patting her hair. "The nit nurse is here."

Rats, thought Henry. He'd hardly started. Slowly he stood up.

Everyone pushed and shoved to be first in line. Then a few children remembered what they were lining up for and stampeded towards the back. Horrid Henry saw his chance and took it.

He charged through the squabbling children, brushing against everyone as fast as he could.

LEAP!

Scratch! Scratch!

LEAP!

Scratch! Scratch!

LEAP!

Scratch! Scratch!

"Henry!" shouted Miss Battle-Axe. "Stay in at playtime. Now go to the end of the queue. The rest of you, stop this nonsense at once!"

Moody Margaret had fought longest and hardest to be first. Proudly she presented her head to Nitty Nora.

"I certainly don't have nits," she said.

Nitty Nora stuck the comb in.

"Nits!" she announced, stuffing a nit note into Margaret's hand.

For once Margaret was too shocked to speak.

"But . . . but . . ." she gasped.

Tee-hee, thought Henry. Now he wouldn't be the only one.

"Next," said Nitty Nora.

She stuck the comb in Rude Ralph's greasy hair.

"Nits!" she announced.

"Nit-face," hissed Horrid Henry, beside himself with glee.

"Nits!" said Nitty Nora, poking her comb into Lazy Linda's mop.

"Nits!" said Nitty Nora, prodding Greedy Graham's frizzy hair.

"Nits, nits, nits, nits, nits!" she continued, pointing at Weepy William, Clever Clare, Sour Susan, Beefy Bert and Dizzy Dave.

Then Nitty Nora beckoned to Miss Battle-Axe.

"Teachers too," she ordered.

Miss Battle-Axe's jaw dropped.

"I have been teaching for twenty-five years and I have never had nits," she said. "Don't waste your time checking *me*."

Nitty Nora ignored her protests and stuck in the comb.

"Hmmn," she said, and whispered in Miss Battle-Axe's ear.

"NO!" howled Miss Battle-Axe.

"NOOOOOOOOOO!" Then she joined the line of weeping, wailing children clutching their nit notes.

At last it was Henry's turn.

Nitty Nora stuck her comb into Henry's tangled hair and dragged it along his scalp. She combed again. And again. And again.

"No nits," said Nitty Nora. "Keep up the good work, young man."

"I sure will!" said Henry.

Horrid Henry skipped home waving his certificate.

"Look, Peter," crowed Henry. "I'm nit-free!"

Perfect Peter burst into tears.

"I'm not," he wailed.

"Hard luck," said Horrid Henry.

2

HORRID HENRY AND THE FANGMANGLER

Horrid Henry snatched his skeleton bank and tried to twist open the trap door. Mum was taking him to Toy Heaven tomorrow. At last Henry would be able to buy the toy of his dreams: a Dungeon Drink kit. Ha ha ha – the tricks he'd play on his family, substituting their drinks for Dungeon stinkers.

Best of all, Moody Margaret would be green with envy. She wanted a

Dungeon Drink kit too, but she didn't have any money. He'd have one first, and no way was Margaret ever going to play with it. Except for buying the occasional sweet and a few comics, Henry had been saving his money for weeks.

Perfect Peter peeked round the door.

"I've saved £7.53," said Peter proudly, jingling his piggy bank. "More than enough to buy my nature kit. How much do you have?"

"Millions," said Henry.

Perfect Peter gasped.

"You do not," said Peter. "Do you?"

Henry shook his bank. A thin rattle came from within.

"That doesn't sound like millions," said Peter.

"That's 'cause five pound notes don't rattle, stupid," said Henry.

"Mum! Henry called me stupid," shrieked Peter.

"Stop being horrid, Henry!" shouted Mum.

Horrid Henry gave the lid of his bank a final yank and spilled the contents on to the floor.

A single, solitary five pence coin rolled out.

Henry's jaw dropped. He grabbed the bank and fumbled around inside. It was empty.

"I've been robbed!" howled Horrid Henry. "Where's my money? Who stole my money?"

Mum ran into the room.

"What's all this fuss?"

"Peter stole my money!" screamed Henry. He glared at his brother. "Just wait until I get my hands on you, you little thief, I'll —"

"No one stole your money, Henry," said Mum. "You've spent it all on sweets and comics."

"I have not!" shrieked Henry.

Mum pointed at the enormous pile of comics and sweet wrappers littering the floor of Henry's bedroom.

"What's all that then?" asked Mum.

Horrid Henry stopped shrieking. It was true. He *had* spent all his pocket money on comics and sweets. He just hadn't noticed.

"It's not fair!" he screamed.

"I saved all *my* pocket money, Mum," said Perfect Peter. "After all, a penny saved is a penny earned."

Mum smiled at him. "Well done, Peter. Henry, let this be a lesson to you."

"I can't wait to buy my nature kit," said Perfect Peter. "You should have saved your money like I did, instead of wasting it, Henry."

Henry growled and sprang at Peter. He was an Indian warrior scalping a settler.

"YOWWWW!" squealed Peter.

"Henry! Stop it!" shouted Mum. "Say sorry to Peter."

"I'm not sorry!" screamed Henry. "I want my money!"

"Any more nonsense from you, young man, and we won't be going to Toy Heaven," said Mum.

Henry scowled.

"I don't care," he muttered. What was the point of going to Toy Heaven if he couldn't buy any toys?

Horrid Henry lay on his bedroom floor kicking sweet wrappers. That Dungeon Drink kit cost £4.99. He had to get some money by tomorrow. The question was, how?

He could steal Peter's money. That was tempting, as he knew the secret place in Peter's cello case where Peter hid his bank. Wouldn't that be fun when Peter discovered his money was gone? Henry smiled.

On second thought, perhaps not. Mum and Dad would be sure to suspect Henry, especially if he suddenly had money and Peter didn't.

He could sell some of his comics to Moody Margaret.

"No!" shrieked Henry, clutching his comics to his chest. Not his precious comics. There *had* to be another way.

Then Henry had a wonderful, spectacular idea. It was so superb that he did a wild war dance for joy. That Dungeon Drink kit was as good as his. And, better still, Peter would give him all the money he needed. Henry chortled. This would be as easy as taking sweets from a baby . . . and a lot more fun.

Horrid Henry strolled down the hall to Peter's room. Peter was having a meeting of the Best Boys Club (motto: Can I help?) with his friends Tidy Ted, Spotless Sam and Goody-Goody Gordon. What luck. More money for him. Henry smiled as he put his ear to the keyhole and listened to them discussing their good deeds.

"I helped an old lady cross the road

and I ate all my vegetables," said Perfect Peter.

"I kept my room tidy all week," said Tidy Ted.

"I scrubbed the bath without being asked," said Spotless Sam.

"I never once forgot to say please and thank you," said Goody-Goody Gordon.

Henry pushed past the barricades and burst into Peter's room.

"Password!" screeched Perfect Peter.

"Vitamins," said Horrid Henry.

"How did you know?" said Tidy Ted, staring open-mouthed at Henry.

"Never you mind," said Henry, who was not a master spy for nothing. "I don't suppose any of you know about Fangmanglers?"

The boys looked at one another.

"What are they?" asked Spotless Sam.

"Only the slimiest, scariest, most horrible and frightening monsters in the whole world," said Henry. "And I know where to find one."

"Where?" said Goody-Goody Gordon.

"I'm not going to tell you," said Horrid Henry.

"Oh please!" said Spotless Sam.

Henry shook his head and lowered his voice.

"Fangmanglers only come out at night," whispered Henry. "They slip into the shadows then sneak out and . . . BITE YOU!" he suddenly shrieked.

The Best Boys Club members gasped with fright.

"I'm not scared," said Peter. "And I've never heard of a Fangmangler."

"That's because you're too young," said Henry. "Grown-ups don't tell you about them because they don't want to scare you."

"I want to see it," said Tidy Ted.

"Me too," said Spotless Sam and Goody-Goody Gordon.

Peter hesitated for a moment.

"Is this a trick, Henry?"

"Of course not," said Henry. "And just for that I won't let you come."

"Oh please, Henry," said Peter.

Henry paused.

"All right," he said. "We'll meet in the back garden after dark. But it will cost you two pounds each."

"Two pounds!" they squealed.

"Do you want to see a Fangmangler or don't you?"

Perfect Peter exchanged a look with his friends.

They all nodded.

"Good," said Horrid Henry. "See you at six o'clock. And don't forget to bring your money."

Tee hee, chortled Henry silently.

Eight pounds! He could get a Dungeon Drink kit *and* a Grisly Ghoul Grub box at this rate.

Loud screams came from next-door's garden.

"Give me back my spade!" came Moody Margaret's bossy tones.

"You're so mean, Margaret," squealed Sour Susan's sulky voice. "Well, I won't. It's my turn to dig with it now."

WHACK! THWACK!

"WAAAAAAA!"

Eight pounds is nice, thought Horrid Henry, but twelve is even nicer.

"What's going on?" asked Horrid Henry, smirking as he leapt over the wall.

"Go away, Henry!" shouted Moody Margaret.

"Yeah, Henry," echoed Sour Susan, wiping away her tears. "We don't want you."

"All right," said Henry. "Then I won't tell you about the Fangmangler I've found."

"We don't want to know about it," said Margaret, turning her back on him.

"That's right," said Susan.

"Well then, don't blame me when the Fangmangler sneaks over the wall and rips you to pieces and chews up your guts," said Horrid Henry. He turned to go.

The girls looked at one another.

"Wait," ordered Margaret.

"Yeah?" said Henry.

"You don't scare me," said Margaret.

"Prove it then," said Henry.

"How?" said Margaret.

"Be in my garden at six o'clock tonight and I'll show you the Fangmangler. But it will cost you two pounds each."

"Forget it," said Margaret. "Come on, Susan."

"Okay," said Henry quickly. "One pound each."

"No," said Margaret.

"And your money back if the Fangmangler doesn't scare you," said Henry.

Moody Margaret smiled.

"It's a deal," she said.

When the coast was clear, Horrid Henry crept into the bushes and hid a bag containing his supplies: an old, torn T-shirt, some filthy trousers and

a jumbo-sized bottle of ketchup.
Then he sneaked back into the house
and waited for dark.

"Thank you, thank you, thank you,
thank you," said Horrid Henry,
collecting two pounds from each
member of the Best Boys Club.
Henry placed the money carefully in
his skeleton bank. Boy, was he rich!

Moody Margaret and Sour Susan
handed over one pound each.

"Remember Henry, we get our
money back if we aren't scared,"
hissed Moody Margaret.

"Shut up, Margaret," said Henry.
"I'm risking my life and all you can
think about is money. Now
everyone, wait here, don't move and
don't talk," he whispered. "We have
to surprise the Fangmangler. If

not . . ." Henry paused and drew his fingers across his throat. "I'm a goner. I'm going off now to hunt for the monster. When I find him, and if it's safe, I'll whistle twice. Then everyone come, as quietly as you can. But be careful!"

Henry disappeared into the black darkness of the garden.

For a long long moment there was silence.

"This is stupid," said Moody Margaret.

Suddenly, a low, moaning growl echoed through the moonless night.

"What was that?" said Spotless Sam nervously.

"Henry? Are you all right, Henry?" squeaked Perfect Peter.

The low moaning growl turned into a snarl.

THRASH! CRASH!

"HELP! HELP! THE FANGMANGLER'S AFTER ME! RUN FOR YOUR LIVES!" screamed Horrid Henry, smashing through the bushes. His T-shirt and trousers were torn. There was blood everywhere.

The Best Boys Club screamed and ran.

Sour Susan screamed and ran.

Moody Margaret screamed and ran.

Horrid Henry screamed and . . . stopped.

He waited until he was alone. Then

Horrid Henry wiped some ketchup from his face, clutched his bank and did a war dance round the garden, whooping with joy.

"Money! Money! Money! Money! Money!" he squealed, leaping and stomping. He danced and he pranced, he twirled and he whirled. He was so busy dancing and cackling he didn't notice a shadowy shape slip into the garden behind him.

"Money! Money! Money! Mine! Mine –" he broke off. What was that noise? Horrid Henry's throat tightened.

"Nah," he thought. "It's nothing."

Then suddenly a dark shape leapt out of the bushes and let out a thunderous roar.

Horrid Henry shrieked with terror. He dropped his money and ran for his life. The Thing scooped up his bank and slithered over the wall.

Horrid Henry did not stop running until he was safely in his room with the door shut tight and barricaded. His heart pounded.

There really is a Fangmangler, he thought, trembling. And now it's after *me*.

Horrid Henry hardly slept a wink. He started awake at every squeak and creak. He shook and he shrieked. Henry had such a bad night that he slept in quite late the next morning, tossing and turning.

FIZZ! POP! GURGLE! BANG!

Henry jerked awake. What was that? He peeked his head out from under the duvet and listened.

FIZZ! POP! GURGLE! BANG!

Those fizzing and popping noises seemed to be coming from next door.

Henry ran to the window and pulled open the curtains. There was Moody Margaret sitting beside a large Toy Heaven bag. In front of her was . . . a Dungeon Drink kit. She saw him, smiled, and raised a glass of bubbling black liquid.

"Want a Fangmangler drink, Henry?" asked Margaret sweetly.

3

HORRID HENRY'S SCHOOL TRIP

"Don't forget my packed lunch for the school trip," shouted Horrid Henry for the tenth time. "I want crisps, biscuits, chocolate, and a fizzywizz drink."

"No way, Henry," said Dad grimly, slicing carrots. "I'm making you a healthy, nutritious lunch."

"But I don't want a healthy lunch," howled Henry. "I like sweets!"

"Sweets, yuck," said Perfect Peter.

He peeked in his lunch box.

"Oh boy, an apple!" said Peter. "And egg and cress on brown bread with the crusts on! And carrot and celery sticks, my favourite! Thank you so much, Dad. Henry, if you don't eat healthy food, you'll never grow big and strong."

"Oh yeah," said Henry. "I'll show you how big and strong I am, you little pipsqueak," he added, springing at Peter. He was a boa constrictor throttling his prey.

"Uggghhhh," choked Peter.

"Stop being horrid, Henry!" shouted Mum. "Or there will be no school trip for you."

Henry let Peter go. Horrid Henry loved school trips. No work. No assembly. A packed lunch. A chance to fool around all day. What could be better?

"I'm going to the Frosty Freeze Ice Cream factory," said Henry. "Free ice creams for everyone. Yippee!"

Perfect Peter made a face. "I don't like ice cream," he said. "My class is going somewhere much better – our Town Museum. And Mum's coming to help."

"I'd rather be boiled alive and eaten by cannibals than go to that boring old dump," said Horrid Henry, shuddering. Mum had dragged him there once. Never again.

Then Henry noticed Peter's T-shirt. It was exactly the same as his, purple striped with gold stars.

"Tell Peter to stop copying what I wear to school!" screamed Henry.

"It doesn't matter, Henry," said Mum. "You're going on different trips. No one will notice."

"Just keep out of my way, Peter," snarled Henry. "I don't want anyone to think we're related."

Horrid Henry's class buzzed with excitement as they scrambled to be first on the bus.

"I've got crisps!" shouted Dizzy Dave.

"I've got biscuits!" shouted Anxious Andrew.

"I've got toffee and chocolate and lollies and three fizzywizzes!" shouted Greedy Graham.

"WAAAA," wailed Weepy
William. "I forgot my packed lunch."

"Quiet!" ordered Miss Battle-Axe
as the bus started moving. "Sit still
and behave. No eating on the bus.
William, stop weeping."

"I need a wee!" shouted Lazy
Linda.

"Well, you'll have to wait,"
snapped Miss Battle-Axe.

Horrid Henry had trampled his
way to the window seats at the back
next to Rude Ralph and Greedy
Graham. He liked those seats best.
Miss Battle-Axe couldn't see him, and
he could make faces at all the people
in the cars behind him.

Henry and Ralph rolled down the
window and chanted:

"Beans, beans, good for the heart,
The more you eat, the more you –"
"HENRY!" bellowed Miss

Battle-Axe. "Turn around and face
forward NOW!"

"I need a wee!" shouted Dizzy
Dave.

"Look what I've got, Henry," said
Greedy Graham, holding a bulging
bag of sweets.

"Gimme some," said Henry.

"And me," said Rude Ralph.

The three boys stuffed their faces
with sweets.

"Ugh, a green lime," said Henry,
taking the sticky sweet out of his
mouth. "Eeech." He flicked the sweet
away.

PING!

The sweet landed on Moody
Margaret's neck.

"Ow," said Margaret.

She turned round and glared at
Henry.

"Stop it, Henry!" she snarled.

"I didn't do anything," said Henry.

PING!

A sweet landed in Sour Susan's hair.

PING!

A sweet stuck on Anxious Andrew's new jumper.

"Henry's throwing sweets!" shouted Margaret.

Miss Battle-Axe turned round.

"Henry! Sit next to me," she said.

"I needed a wee!" wailed Weepy William.

Finally, the bus drove up to the Frosty Freeze Factory. A gigantic, delicious-looking ice cream cone loomed above it.

"We're here!" shouted Henry.

"You scream! I scream! We all scream for ice cream!" shrieked the children as the bus stopped outside the gate.

"Why are we waiting here?" yelled Greedy Graham. "I want my ice creams now!"

Henry stuck his head out of the window. The gates were chained shut. A large sign read: "CLOSED on Mondays."

Miss Battle-Axe looked pale. "I don't believe this," she muttered.

"Class, there's been a mix-up, and we seem to have come on the wrong day," said Miss Battle-Axe. "But never mind. We'll go to –"

"The Science Museum!" shouted
Clever Clare.

"The zoo!" shouted Dizzy Dave.

"Lazer Zap!" shouted Horrid
Henry.

"No," said Miss Battle-Axe. "Our
Town Museum."

"Ugggghhhhh," groaned the class.

No one groaned louder than
Horrid Henry.

The children left their jackets and
lunch boxes in the packed lunch room,
and then followed the museum guide
to Room 1.

"First we'll see Mr Jones's
collection of rubber bands," said the
guide. "Then our famous display of
door hinges and dog collars through
history. And don't worry, you'll be

seeing our latest acquisitions, soil
from Miss Montague's garden and
the Mayor's baby pictures."

Horrid Henry had to escape.

"I need a wee," said Henry.

"Hurry up then," said Miss
Battle-Axe. "And come straight
back."

The toilets were next to the packed
lunch room.

Henry thought he'd make sure his
lunch was still there. Yup, there it
was, right next to Ralph's.

I wonder what Ralph has got,
thought Henry, staring at Ralph's
packed lunch. No harm in looking.

WOW. Rude Ralph's lunch box
was bursting with crisps, sweets, and
a chocolate spread sandwich on white
bread.

He'll feel sick if he eats all that junk

food, thought Henry. I'd better help him.

It was the work of a moment to swap Ralph's sandwich for Henry's egg and cress.

This certainly isn't very healthy, thought Henry, gazing at Greedy Graham's goodies. I'll do him a favour and exchange a few of my celery sticks for his sweets.

Just look at all those treats, thought Henry, fingering Sour Susan's cakes. She should eat a more balanced meal.

A pack of raisins zipped from Henry's lunch box to Susan's and a sticky bun leapt from Susan's to Henry's.

Tsk tsk, thought Henry, helping himself to Tough Toby's chocolate bar and replacing it with an apple. Too many sweets are bad for the teeth.

That's better, he thought, gazing at his re-packed lunch with satisfaction. Then he strolled back to his class, who were gathered round a glass case.

"This is the soil in which Miss Montague grew her prize-winning vegetables," droned the guide. "She grew marrows, tomatoes, potatoes, leeks –"

"When do we eat?" interrupted Horrid Henry.

"I'm starving," whined Greedy Graham.

"My tummy's rumbling," groaned Rude Ralph.

"When's lunch?" moaned Moody Margaret.

"WE'RE HUNGRY!" wailed the children.

"All right," said Miss Battle-Axe. "We'll eat now."

The class stampeded down the hall and grabbed their lunches. Henry sat in a corner and tucked in.

For a moment there was silence, then the room echoed with howls of dismay.

"Where's my sticky bun?" yelped Sour Susan.

"My sweets are gone!" screamed Greedy Graham.

"What's this? Egg and cress? Yuck!" shouted Rude Ralph, hurling the sandwich at Anxious Andrew.

That did it. The room filled with flying carrot and celery sticks, granola bars, raisins, crusts, and apples. Henry smirked as he wiped the last traces of chocolate from his mouth.

"Stop it! Stop it!" howled Miss
Battle-Axe. "Well done, Henry, for
being the only sensible child. You
may lead us back to see the pieces of
Roman pottery in Room 2."

Horrid Henry walked proudly at
the head of the shuffling, whining
children. Then he noticed the lift at
the far end. A sign read:

STAFF ONLY:

DO NOT ENTER

I wonder where that lift goes,
thought Horrid Henry.

"Stop him!" yelled a guard.

But it was too late.

Henry had dashed to the lift and
pressed the top button.

Up up up he zipped.

Henry found himself in a small
room filled with half-finished
exhibits. On display were lists of

overdue library books, "lightbulbs from 1965 to today," and rows and rows of rocks.

Then, in the corner, Henry actually saw something interesting: a dog's skeleton protected by a drooping blue cord.

Henry looked more closely.

It's just a pile of bones, thought Henry.

He wobbled the blue cord then stood on it.

"Look at me, I'm a tight-rope walker," chortled Horrid Henry, swaying on the blue cord. "I'm the best tight-rope walker in – AGGGHHHH!"

Horrid Henry lost his balance and toppled against the skeleton.

CLITTER-CLATTER! The bones crashed to the ground.

DING DING DING. A burglar alarm began to wail.

Museum guards ran into the room.

Uh-oh, thought Horrid Henry. He slipped between a guard's legs and ran. Behind him he could hear pounding feet.

Henry dashed into a large room filled with road signs, used bus tickets and traffic cones. At the other end of the room Henry saw Peter's class gathered in front of "The Story of the Drain". Oh no. There was Mum.

Henry ducked behind the traffic cones.

Museum guards entered.

"There he is!" shouted one. "The boy in the purple T-shirt with the gold stars."

Henry stood fixed to the spot. He was trapped. Then the guards ran straight past his hiding place. A long arm reached over and plucked Perfect Peter from his group.

"Come with us, you!" snarled the guard. "We're going straight to the Bad Children's Room."

"But . . . but . . ." gasped Peter.

"No ifs or buts!" snapped the guard. "Who's in charge of this child?"

"I am," said Mum. "What's the meaning of this?"

"You come too," ordered the guard.

"But . . . but . . ." gasped Mum.

Shouting and protesting, Mum and Perfect Peter were taken away.

Then Henry heard a familiar booming voice.

"Margaret, that's enough pushing," said Miss Battle-Axe. "No touching, Ralph. Stop weeping, William. Hurry up, everyone! The bus leaves in five minutes. Walk quietly to the exit."

Everyone immediately started running.

Horrid Henry waited until most of the children had charged past then rejoined the group.

"Where have you been, Henry?" snapped Miss Battle-Axe.

"Just enjoying this brilliant museum," said Horrid Henry. "When can we come back?"

4

HORRID HENRY AND THE DINNER GUESTS

FIZZ! POP! GURGLE! BANG!

Horrid Henry sat on the kitchen floor watching his new Dungeon Drink kit brew a bubbly purple potion.

BELCH! CRUNCH! OOZE! SPLAT!

Beside it, a Grisly Ghoul Grub box heaved and spewed some Rotten Crispies.

Dad dashed into the kitchen.

"Want a crisp?" said Henry, smirking.

"No!" said Dad, putting on his apron. "And I've told you before to play with those disgusting kits in your bedroom."

Why Henry's grandmother had bought him those terrible toys for Christmas he would never know.

"Henry, I want you to listen carefully," said Dad, feverishly rolling out pastry. "Mum's new boss and her husband are coming to dinner in an hour. I want total cooperation and perfect behaviour."

"Yeah, yeah," said Henry, his eyes glued to the frothing machine.

Horrid Henry's parents didn't have guests for dinner very often. The last time they did Henry had sneaked downstairs, eaten the entire chocolate cake Dad had baked for dessert and then been sick all over the sofa. The time before that he'd put whoopee cushions on all the guests' seats, bitten Peter, and broken the banister by sliding down it.

PRRRRRP

Dad started getting pots and pans down.

"What are you cooking?" said Perfect Peter, tidying up his stamps.

"Salmon wrapped in pastry with lime and ginger," said Dad, staring at his list.

"Yummy!" said Perfect Peter. "My favourite!"

"Yuck!" said Horrid Henry. "I want pizza. What's for pudding?"

"Chocolate mousse," said Dad.

"Can I help?" said Peter.

"Of course," said Mum, smiling. "You can pass round the nuts and crisps when Mr and Mrs Mossy arrive."

Nuts? Crisps? Henry's ears perked up.

"I'll help too," said Henry.

Mum looked at him. "We'll see," she said.

"I don't think Henry should pass round the nuts," said Peter. "He'll only eat them himself."

"Shut up, Peter," snarled Henry.

"Mum! Henry told me to shut up!" wailed Peter.

"Henry! Stop being horrid," muttered Dad, grating ginger and squeezing limes.

While Dad rolled up salmon in pastry, Mum dashed about setting the table with the best china.

"Hey! You haven't set enough places," said Henry. "You've only set the table for four."

"That's right," said Mum. "Mrs Mossy, Mr Mossy, Dad and me."

"What about me?" said Henry.

"And me?" said Peter.

"This is a grown-ups' party," said Mum.

"You want me . . . to go . . . to bed?" Henry stuttered. "I'm not . . . eating with you?"

"No," said Dad.

"It's not fair!" shrieked Henry. "What am I having for supper then?"

"A cheese sandwich," said Dad. "We've got to get ready for the guests. I'm already two minutes behind my schedule."

"I'm not eating this swill!" shrieked Henry, shoving the sandwich off his plate. "I want pizza!"

"That's all right, Dad," said Peter, tucking into his sandwich. "I understand that grown-ups need to be by themselves sometimes."

Henry lunged at Peter. He was a cannibal trussing his victim for the pot.

"AAARGHH!" shrieked Peter.

"That's it, Henry, go to bed!" shouted Mum.

"I won't!" screamed Henry. "I want chocolate mousse!"

"Go upstairs and stay upstairs!" shouted Mum.

Ding dong!

"Aaagh!" squealed Dad. "They're early! I haven't finished the mousse yet."

Horrid Henry stomped upstairs to his bedroom and slammed the door.

He was so angry he could hardly speak. The injustice of it all. Why should he go to bed while Mum and Dad were downstairs having fun and eating chocolate mousse? The delicious smell of melting chocolate wafted into his nostrils. Henry's tummy rumbled. If Mum and Dad thought he'd stay in bed while they all had fun downstairs they had rocks for brains.

SCREEEECH! SCREEEECH!

Perfect Peter must be playing his cello for Mum and Dad and the guests. Which meant . . . Horrid Henry smiled. The coast was clear. Hello, nuts, here I come, thought Henry.

Henry tip-toed downstairs. The screechy-scratchy sounds continued from the sitting room.

Horrid Henry sneaked into the empty kitchen. There were the bowls of nuts and crisps and the drinks all ready to serve.

Cashews, my favourite. I'll just have a few, he thought.

Chomp. Chomp. Chomp.

Hmmn, boy, those nuts were good. Irresistible, really, thought Henry. A few more would go down a treat. And, if he poured the remaining nuts into a smaller bowl, no one would notice how many he'd eaten.

CHOMP! CHOMP! CHOMP!

Just one more, thought Henry, and that's it.

Horrid Henry swizzled his fingers round the nut bowl.

Uh-oh. There were only three nuts left.

Yikes, thought Henry. Now I'm in trouble.

FIZZ! POP! GURGLE! BANG!
BELCH! CRUNCH! OOZE!
SPLAT!

Horrid Henry looked at his Grisly
Grub box and Dungeon Drink kit
and bopped himself on the head.
What an idiot he was. What better
time to try out his grisly grub than
. . . now?

Henry examined the Rotten
Crispies he'd made earlier. They
looked like crisps, but certainly didn't
taste like them. The only problem
was, what to do with the good crisps?

Yum yum! thought Henry,
crunching crisps as fast as he could.
Then he re-filled the bowl with
Rotten Crispies.

Next, Henry poured two frothing
dungeon drinks into glasses, and put
them on the tray.

Perfect, thought Henry. Now to make some Nasty Nuts to replace all those cashews.

The kitchen door opened. Dad came in.

"What are you doing, Henry? I told you to go to bed."

"Mum said I could serve the nuts," said Henry, lying shamelessly. Then he grabbed the two bowls and escaped.

The sound of applause came from the sitting room. Perfect Peter bowed modestly.

"Isn't he adorable?" said Mrs Mossy.

"And so talented," said Mr Mossy.

"Hello, Mr and Mrs Bossy," said Henry.

Mum looked horrified.

"Mossy, not Bossy, dear" said Mum.

"But that's what *you* call them, Mum," said Henry, smiling sweetly.

"Henry is just going to bed," said Mum, blushing.

"No I wasn't," said Henry. "I was going to serve the nuts and crisps. Don't you remember?"

"Oooh, I love nuts," said Mrs Mossy.

"I told you to stay upstairs," hissed Mum.

"Muuuum," wailed Peter. "You said I could serve the guests."

"You can serve the crisps, Peter," said Henry graciously, handing him the bowl of Rotten Crispies. "Would you like a cashew, Mrs Bossy?"

"Mossy!" hissed Mum.

"Ooh, cashews, my favourite," said Mrs Mossy. She plunged her fingers into the mostly empty nut bowl, and finally scooped up the remaining three.

Henry snatched two back.

"You're only supposed to have one nut at a time," he said. "Don't be greedy."

"Henry!" said Mum. "Don't be rude."

"Want a nut?" said Henry, waving

the bowl in front of Mr Mossy.

"Why, yes, I . . ." said Mr Mossy.

But he was too late. Henry had already moved away to serve Mum.

"Want a nut?" he asked.

Mum's hand reached out to take one, but Henry quickly whisked the bowl away.

"Henry!" said Mum.

"Do have some crisps, Mrs Mossy," said Perfect Peter. Mrs Mossy scooped up a large handful of Rotten Crispies and then stuffed them in her mouth.

Her face went purple, then pink, then green.

"BLEEEEECH!" she spluttered, spitting them out all over Mr Mossy.

"Peter, run and get Mrs Mossy something to drink!" shouted Mum.

Peter dashed to the kitchen and brought back a frothing drink.

"Thank you," gasped Mrs Mossy, taking the glass and gulping it down.

"YUCK!" she spluttered, spitting it out. "Are you trying to poison me, you horrible child?" she choked, flailing her arms and crashing into Dad, who had just walked in carrying the drinks tray.

CRASH! SPLASH!

Mum, Dad, Peter, and Mr and Mrs Mossy were soaked.

"Peter, what have you done?" shouted Mum.

Perfect Peter burst into tears and ran out of the room.

"Oh dear, I'm so sorry," said Mum.

"Never mind," said Mrs Mossy, through gritted teeth.

"Sit down, everyone," said Henry. "I'm going to do a show now."

"No," said Mum.

"No," said Dad.

"But Peter did one," howled Henry. "I WANT TO DO A SHOW!"

"All right," said Mum. "But just a quick one."

Henry sang. The guests held their ears.

"Not so loud, Henry," said Mum.

Henry pirouetted, trampling on the guests.

"Ooof," said Mr Mossy, clutching his toe.

"Aren't you finished, Henry?" said Dad.

Henry juggled, dropping both balls on Mrs Mossy's head.

"Ow," said Mrs Mossy.

"Now I'll show you my new karate moves," said Henry.

"NO!" shouted Mum and Dad.

But before anyone could stop him Henry's arms and legs flew out in a mad karate dance.

"HI-YA!" shrieked Henry, knocking into Mr Mossy.

Mr Mossy went flying across the room.

Whoosh! Off flew his toupee.

Click-clack! Out bounced his false teeth.

"Reginald!" gasped Mrs Mossy. "Are you all right? Speak to me!"

"Uggghhh," groaned Mr Mossy.

"Isn't that great?" said Henry. "Who wants to go next?"

"What's that terrible smell?" choked Mrs Mossy.

"Oh no!" screamed Dad. "The salmon is burning!"

Mum and Dad ran into the kitchen, followed by Mr and Mrs Mossy. Smoke poured from the oven. Mum grabbed a tea towel and started whacking the burning salmon.

WHACK! THWACK!

"Watch out!" screamed Dad.

The towel thwacked the bowl of chocolate mousse and sent it crashing to the ground.

SPLAT! There was chocolate mousse on the floor. There was chocolate mousse on the ceiling. And there was chocolate mousse all over Mr and Mrs Mossy, Mum, Dad and Henry.

"Oh no," said Mum, holding her head in her hands. Then she burst into tears. "What are we going to do?"

"Leave it to me, Mum," said Horrid Henry. He marched to the phone.

"Pizza Delight?" he said. "I'd like to order a mega-whopper, please."